I0830737

BULLDOGS

Dale Lazarov, Chas Hunter & Si Arden

BULLDOGS

StickyGraphicNovels.com

Printed and distributed by
ComicMix, LLC.,
71 Hauxhurst Ave. Suite B
Weehawken, NJ 07086.
http://www.comicmix.com

Printed in USA.

Hardcover ISBN: 978-1-939888-61-7

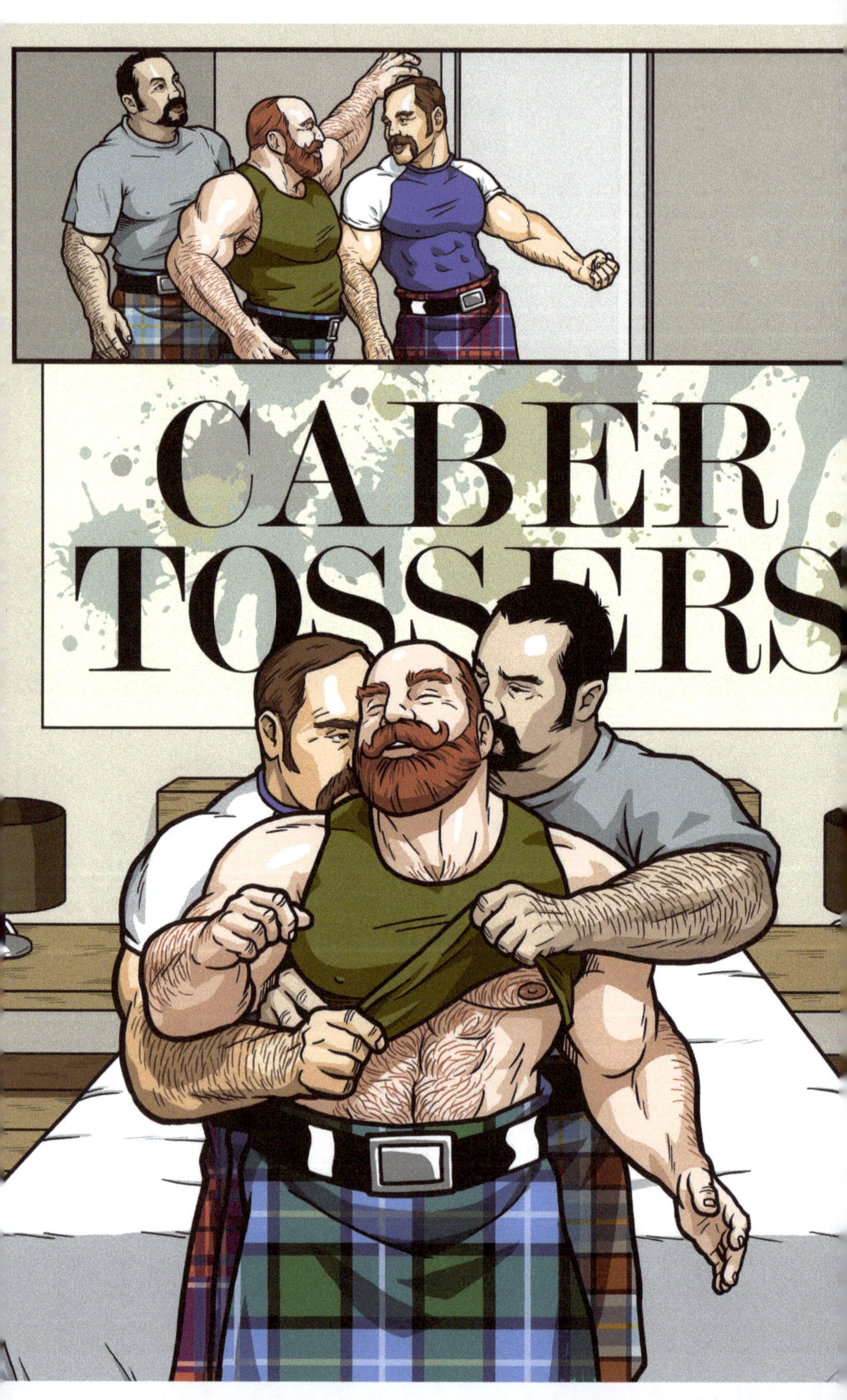

CABER TOSSERS

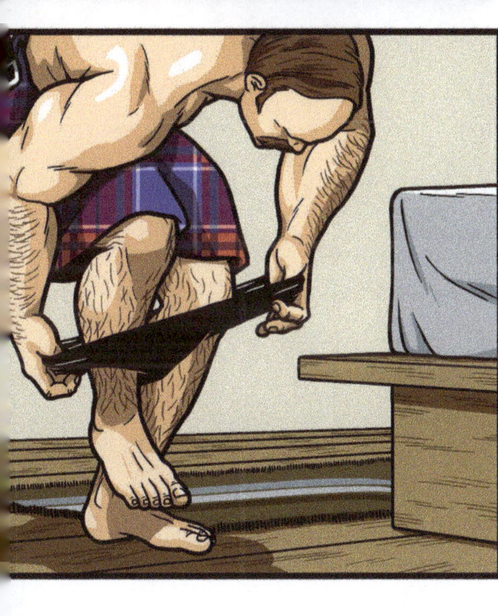

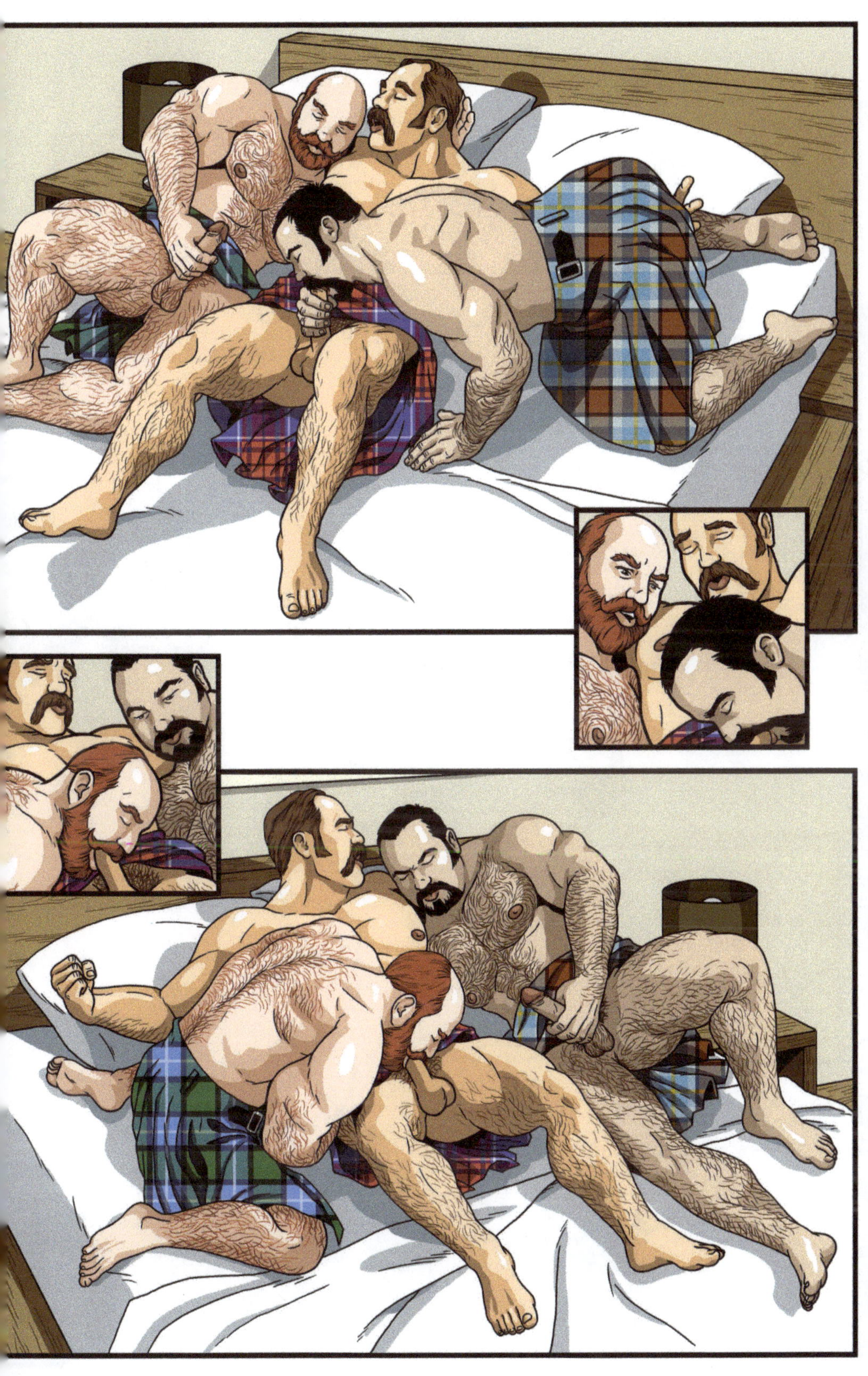

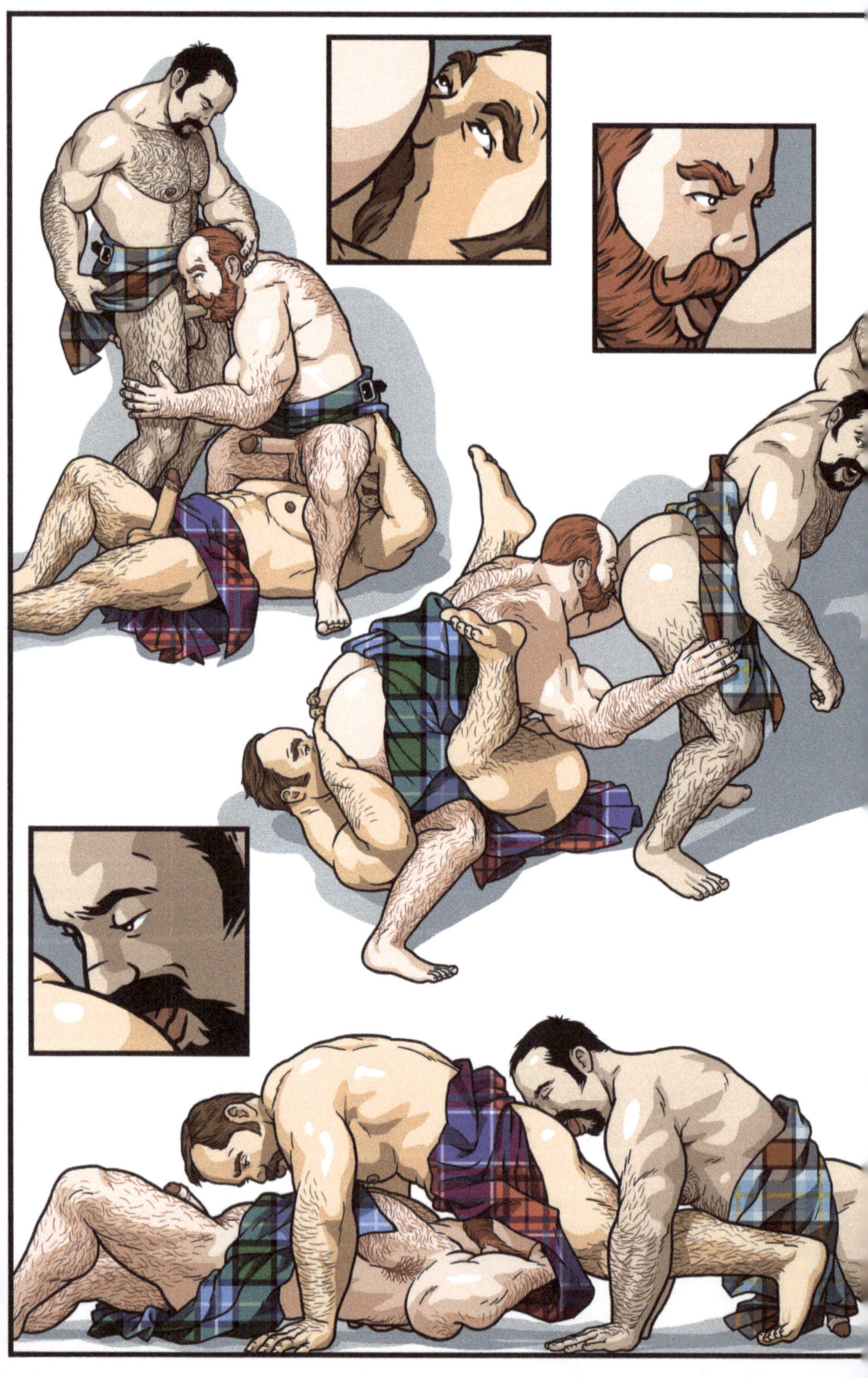

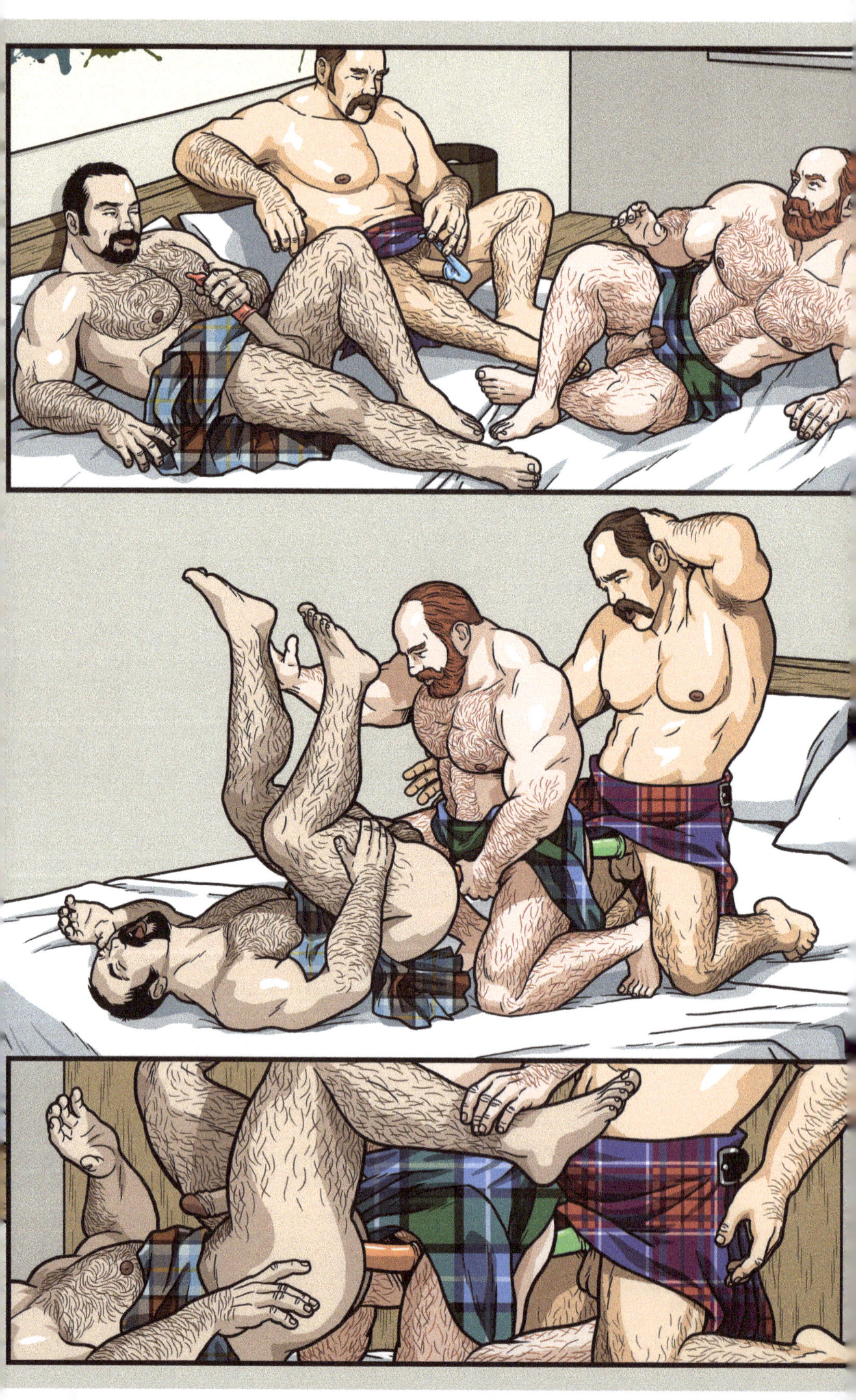

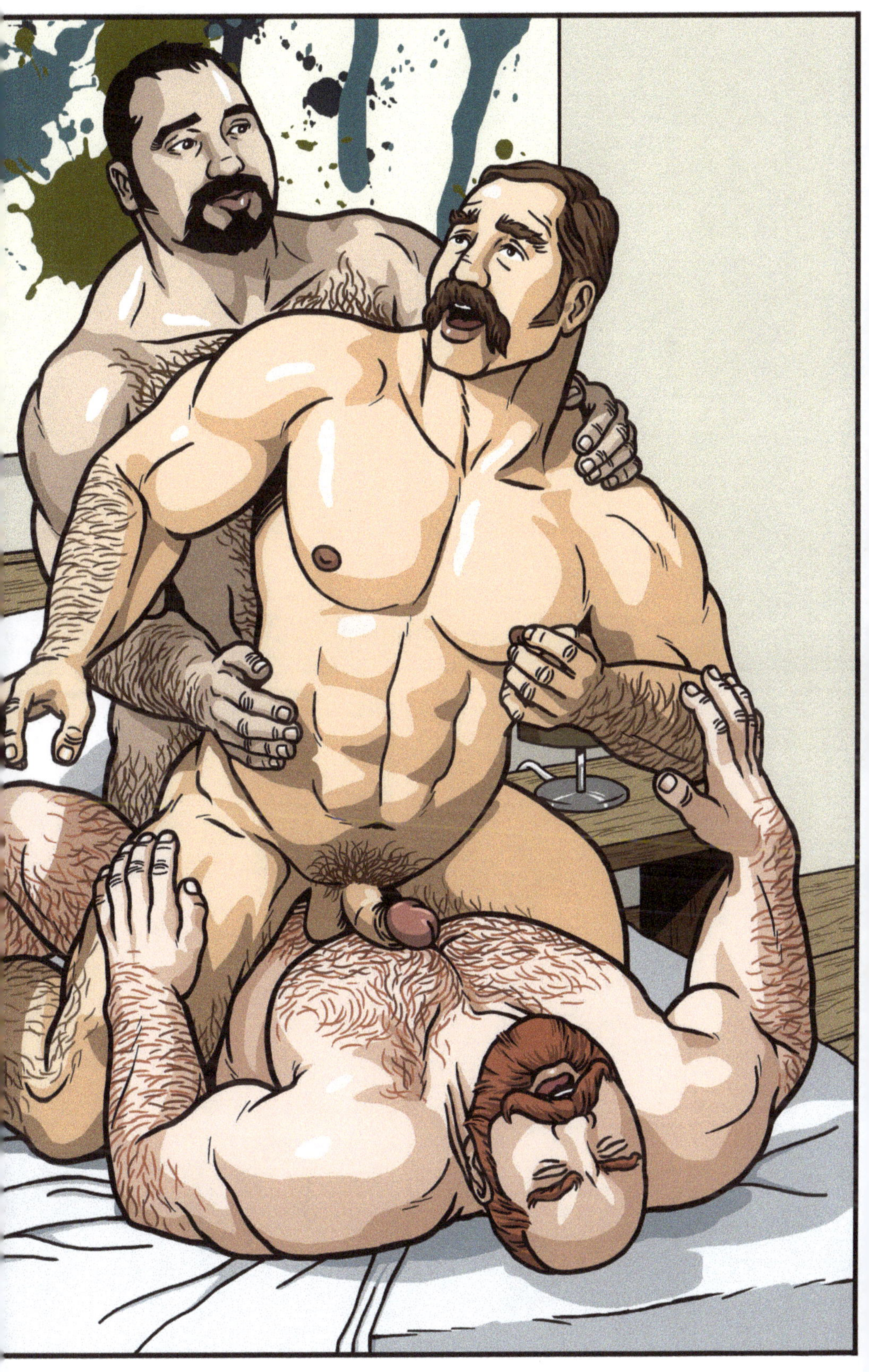

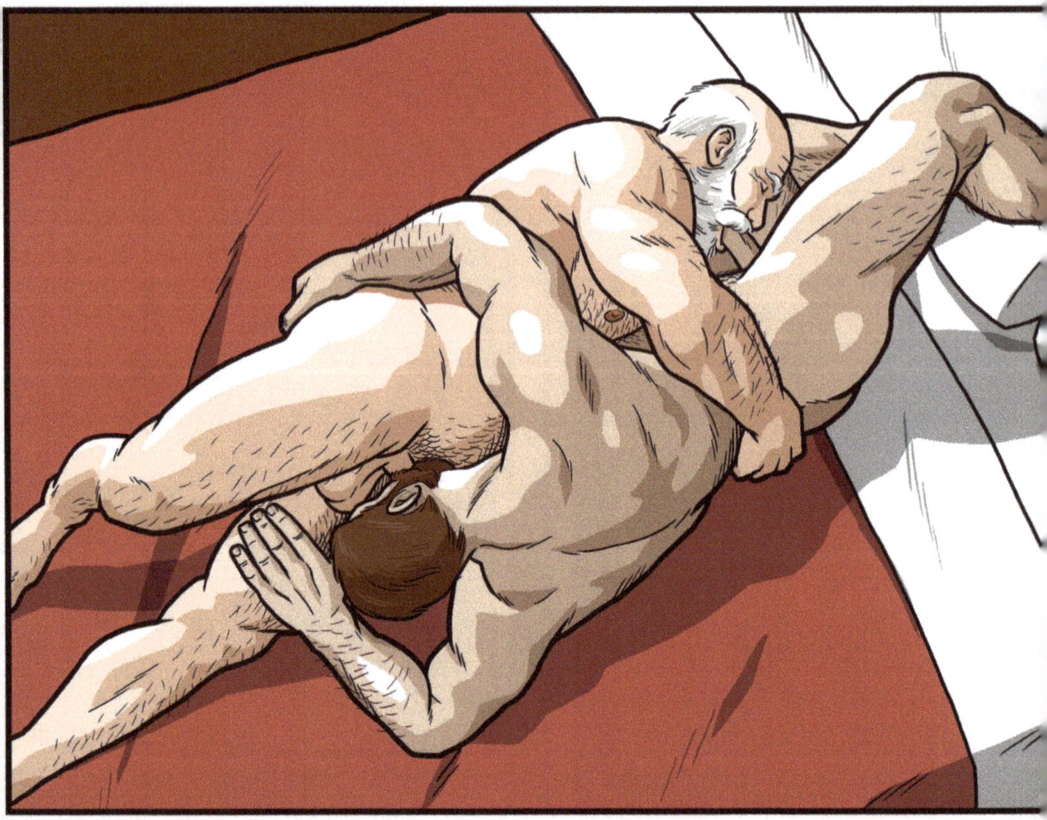

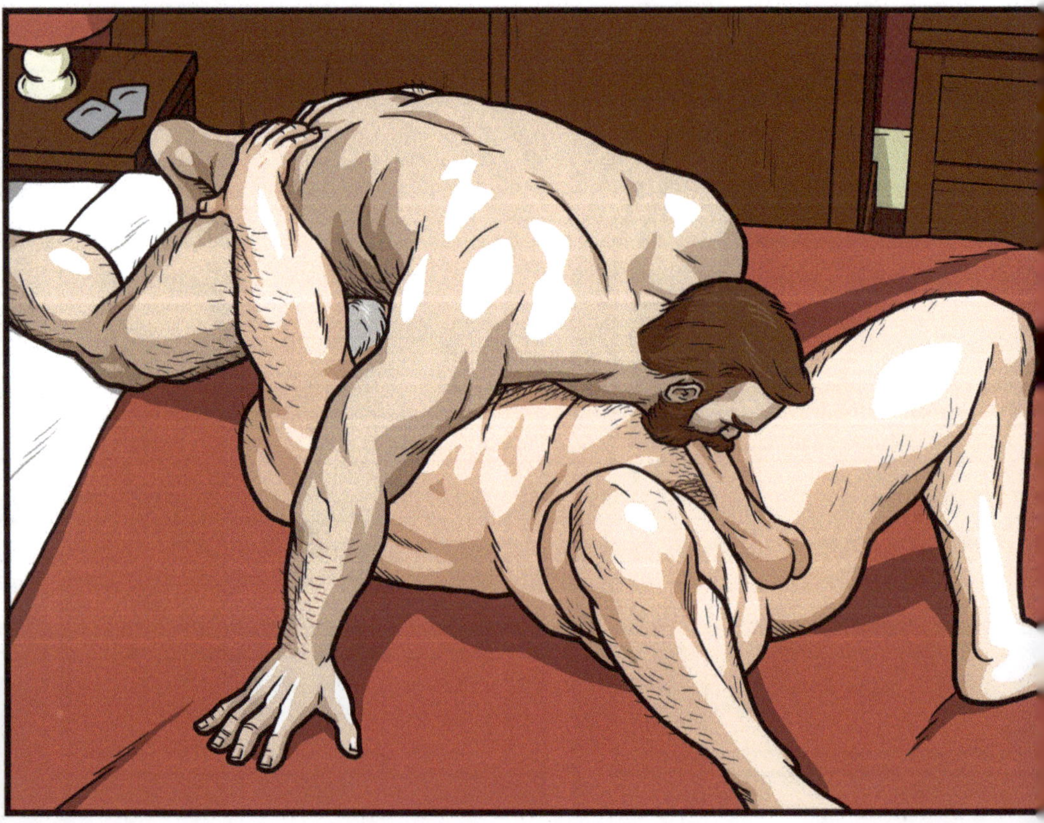

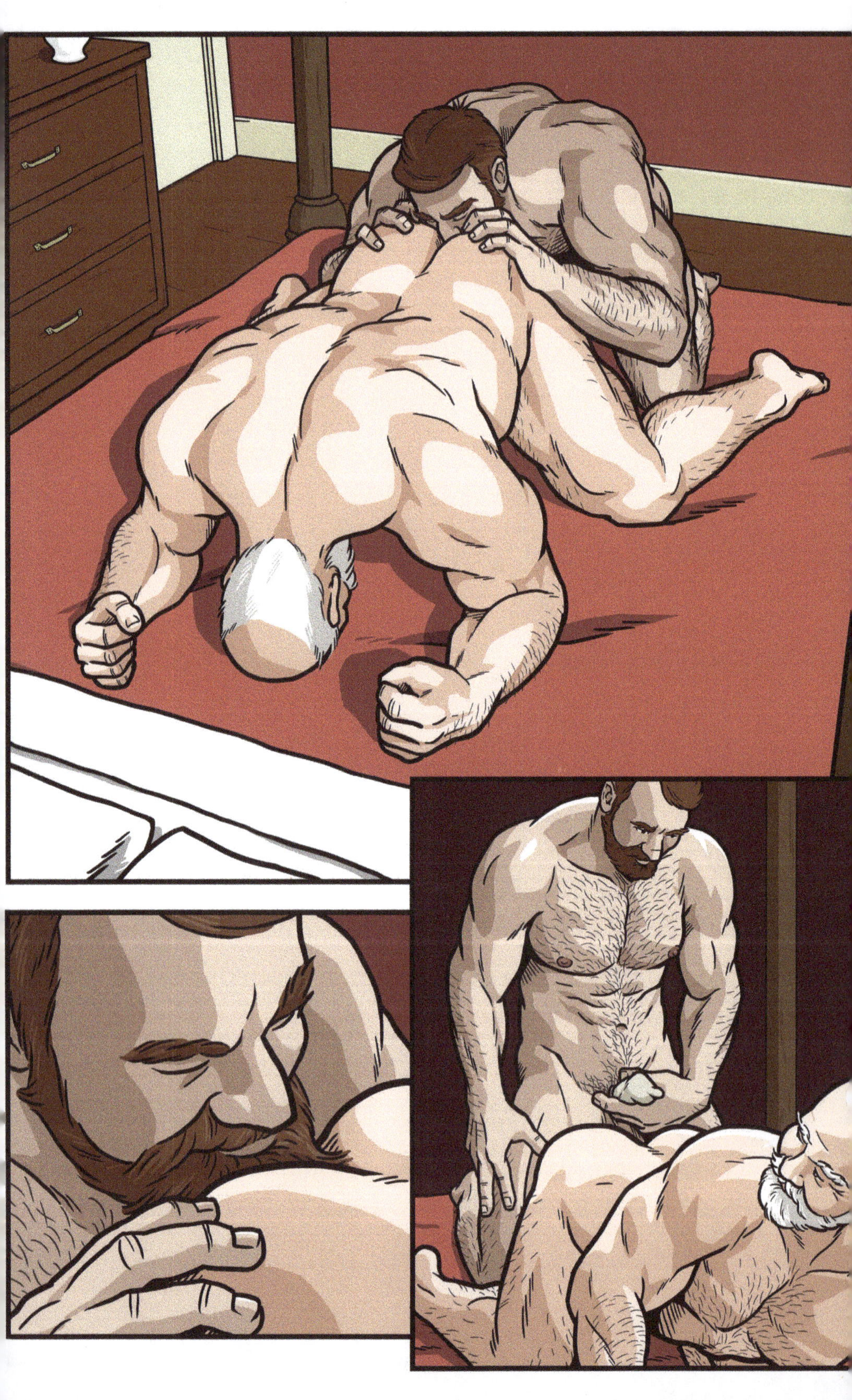

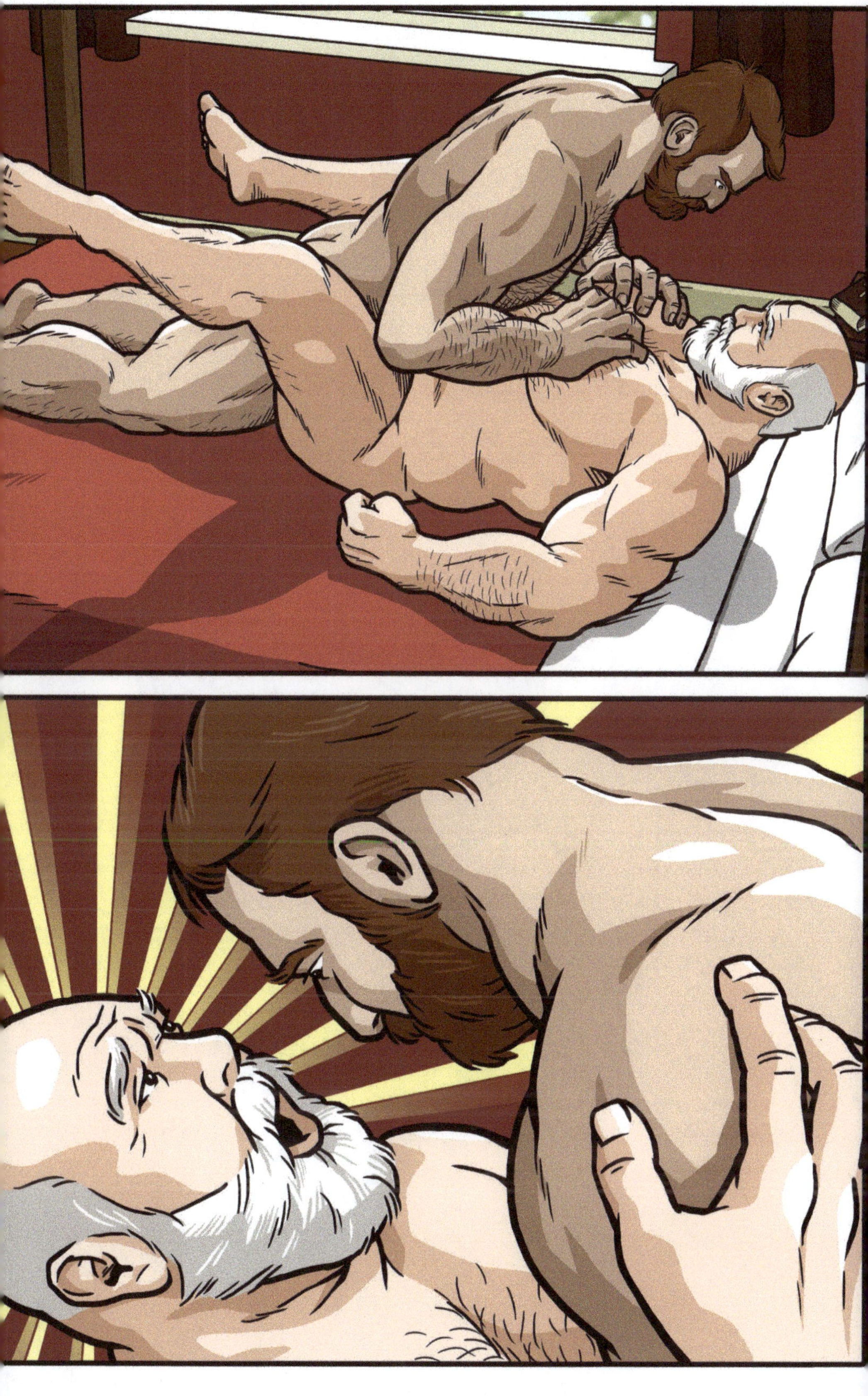

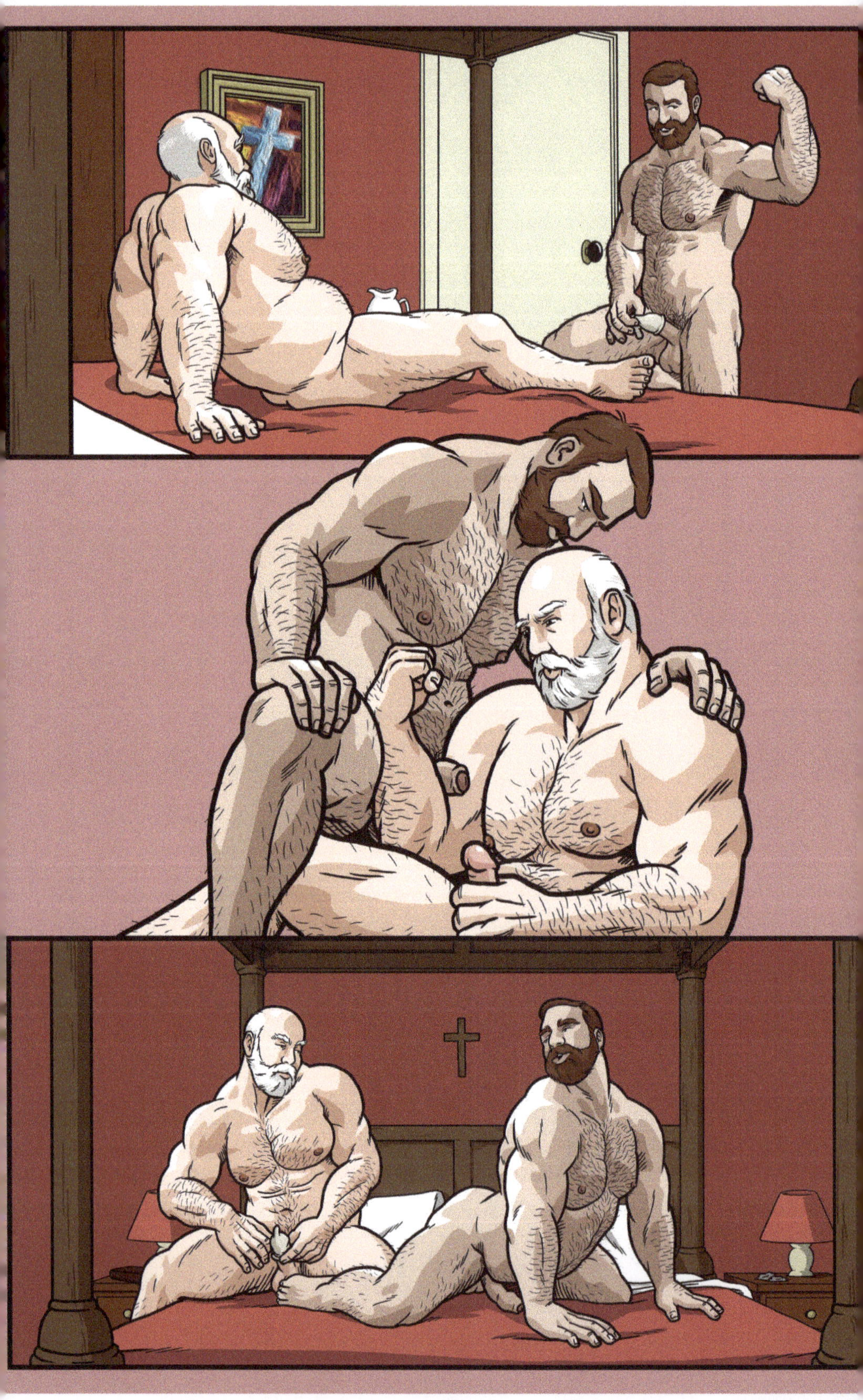

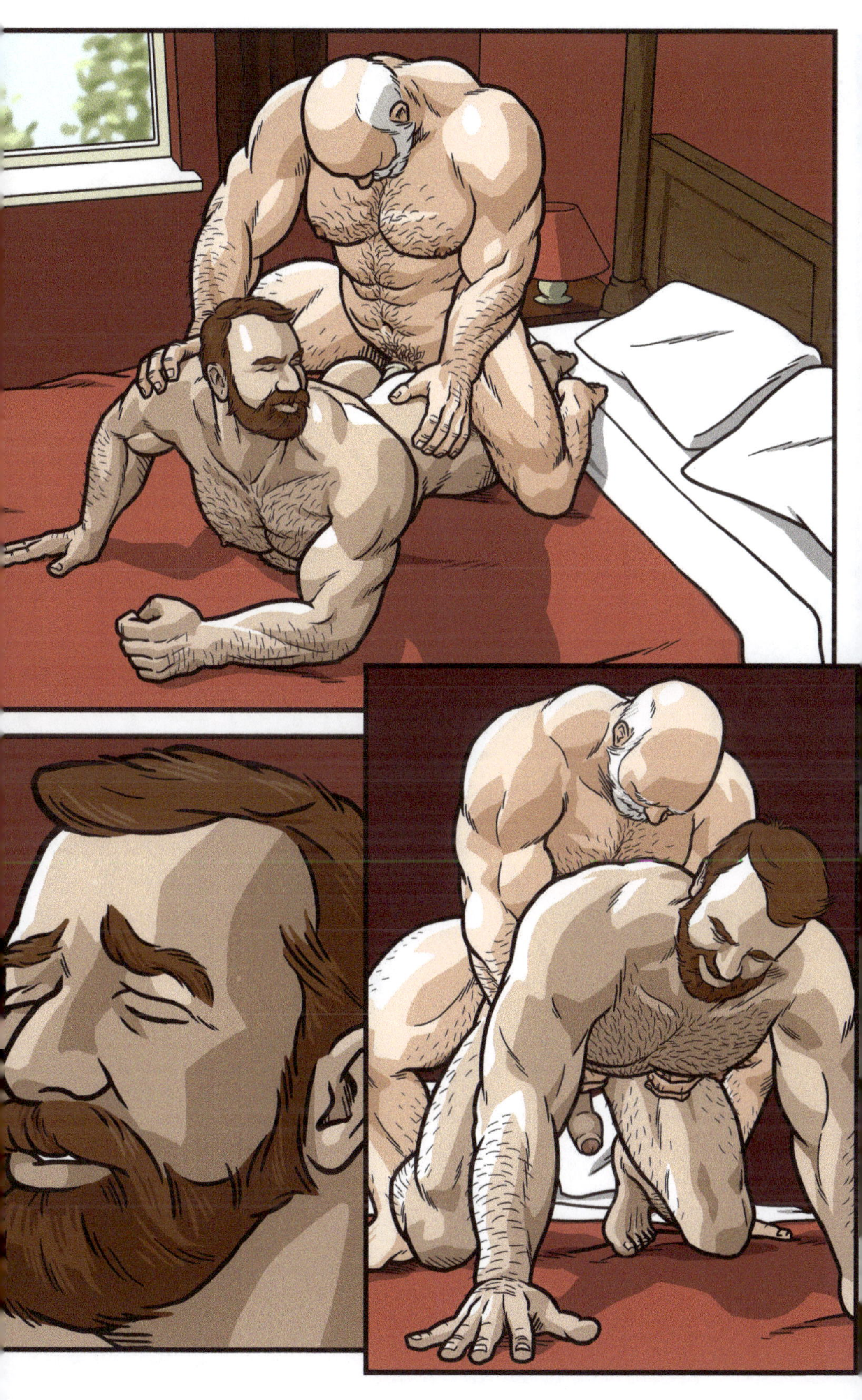

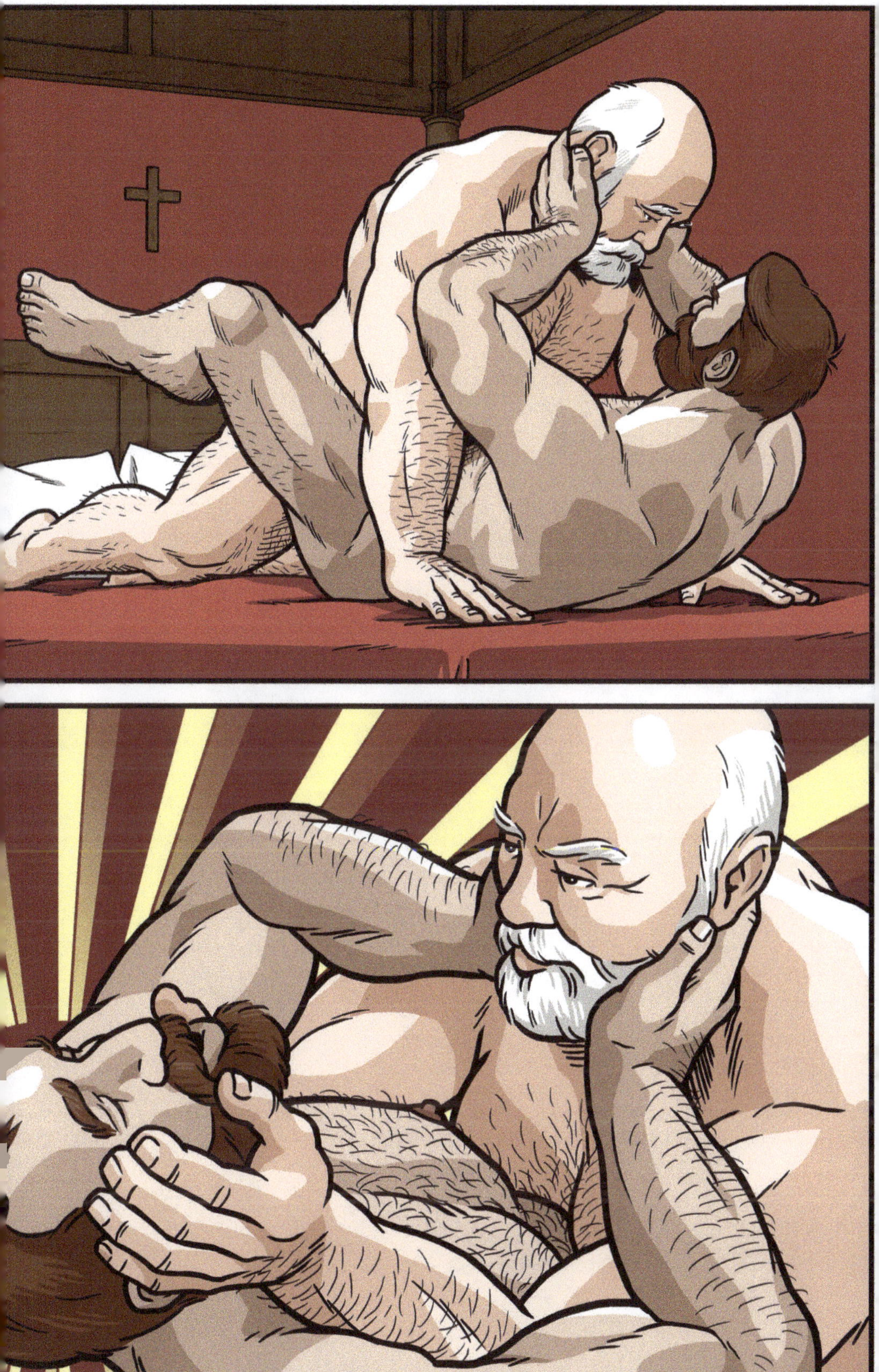

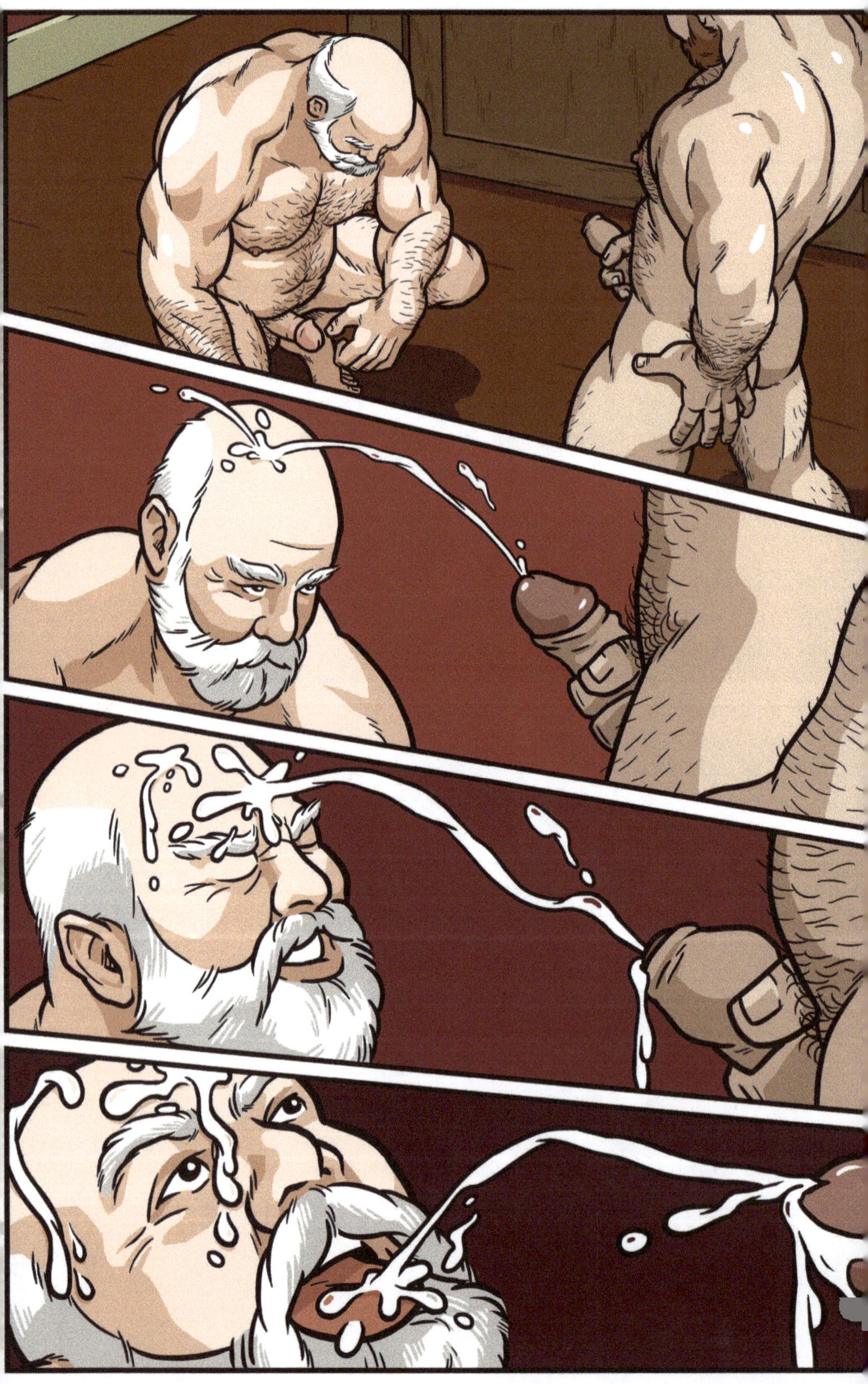

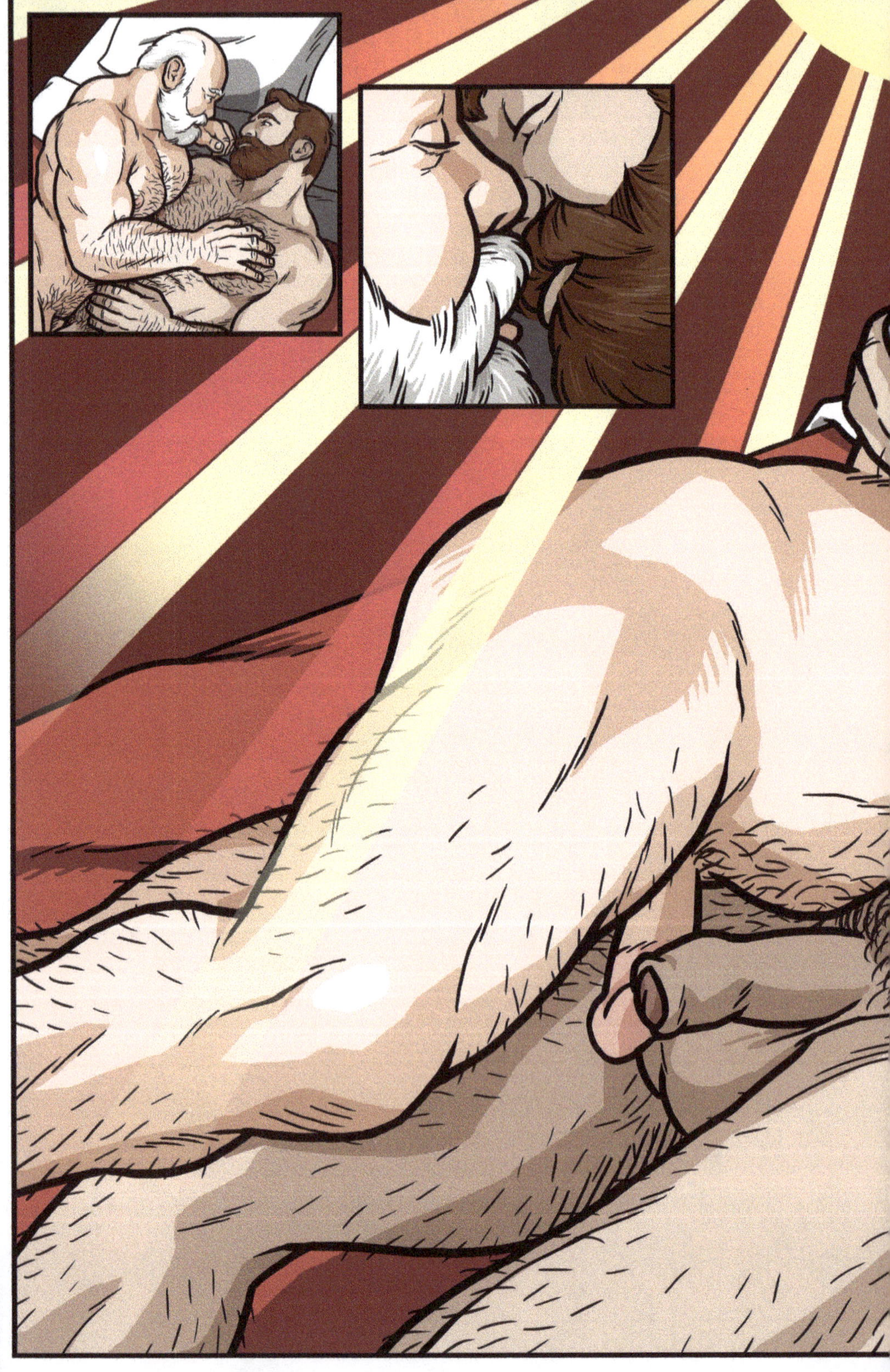

HOT VICAR ON
VICAR ACTION

KINNELL

EXTERMINATE!
EXTERMINATE!

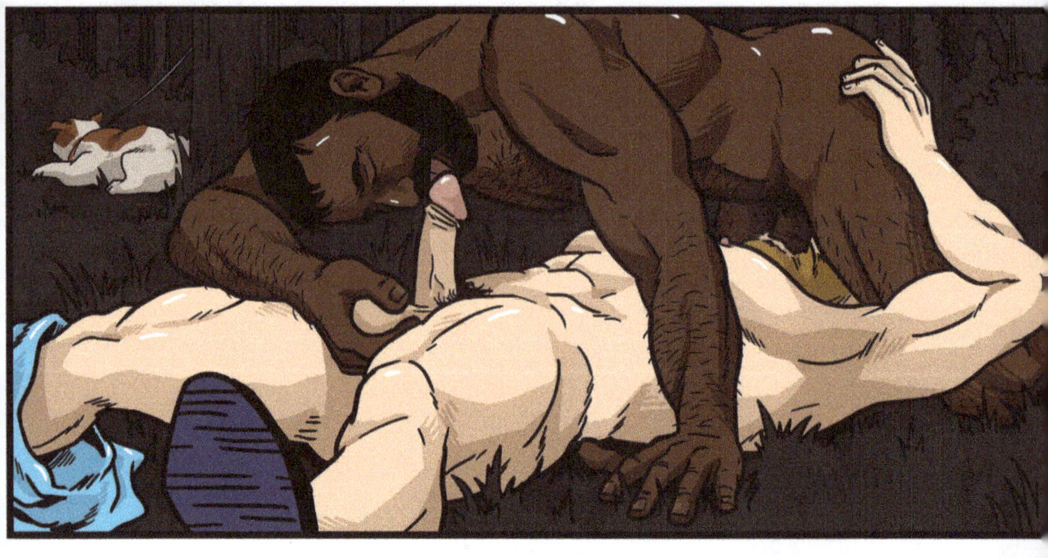

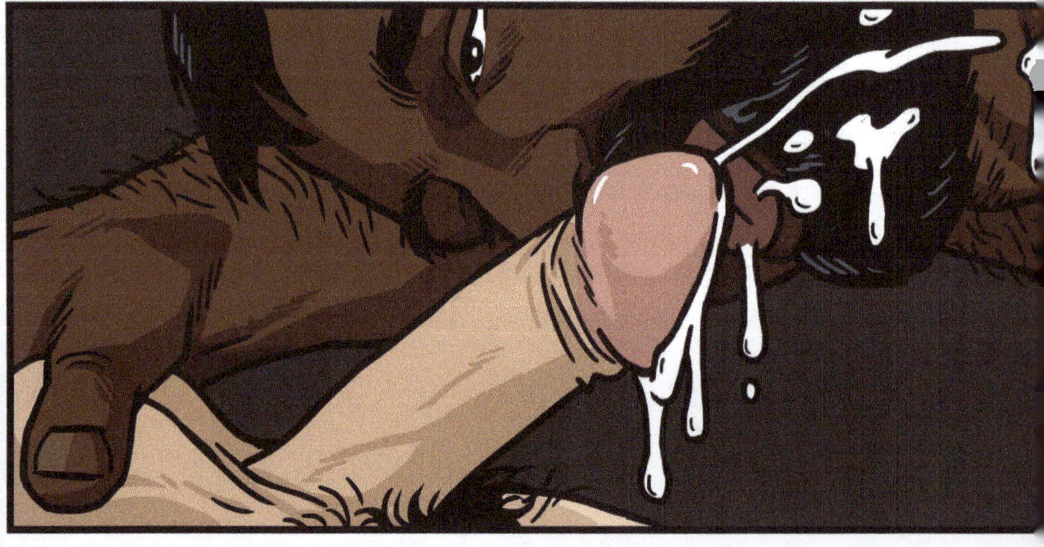

FAIR COP

About The Authors:

Dale Lazarov is the writer, art director and licensor of Sticky Graphic Novels — wordless, gay character-based, sex-positive graphic novels for an international audience. Since 2006, he has collaborated on 12 hardcover Sticky Graphic Novels and 39 digital editions with distinctive and evocative gay comics artists from around the globe. He lives in Chicago.

Chas Hunter studied commercial art at OCAD in Toronto, Canada and Central St. Martins in London, UK. He has worked in the London creative/advertising industry for over 20 years. He's been in group shows in Manchester, Toronto, Denver and Sydney and his current work can be seen online at flux-art.co.uk.

Si Arden has had a passion for art and comics for as long as he can remember. He studied at the University of Plymouth in Devon, UK, where he earned a degree in Fine Art. After leaving the picturesque West Country to move to Birmingham, he worked in the fashion industry for several years before settling in Nottingham, where he recently took a break from employment to concentrate on painting, digital art and working on his portfolio. Si has recently returned to the fashion industry but continues to produce artwork in his spare time.